JACK TH
TAKŁ

ALAN CLIFF

Half author royalties to
Tŷ Gobaith

printed & published by
Gwasg Helygain Ltd
68/70 Kinmel Street, Rhyl, Denbighshire LL18 1AW
01745 331411

Author: Alan Cliff, 2008 ©
Front Cover and Internal Art: Nigel Cliff, 2008 ©
Guest Artist: Roger M. Dilley, 2008 ©
Puzzles: Brenda Wyatt, 2008 ©

ISBN 978-0-9550338-9-6

Printed & Published by:
Gwasg Helygain Ltd., 68/70 Kinmel Street,
Rhyl, Denbighshire LL18 1AW
Tel: 01745 331411 Fax: 01745 331310
Trade enquiries & book orders welcome.
E-mail: info@gwasg.com
Website: www.gwasg.com

British Library Cataloguing-in-Publication Data
A catalogue record for this book is available from the British Library.

www.jackthestationcat.co.uk
Order books online at: www.gwasg.com

Railway 'Jack Days' may be organised.
Please visit the Jack website in the first instance.

Reading guide: 5-8 year olds

HOSBIS PLANT
Tŷ Gobaith
CHILDREN'S HOSPICE

www.tygobaith.org.uk
Tel: 01492 596581

When a parent is told their child will not live to be an adult, it is the start of an agonising journey. A childhood terminal illness challenges every belief, emotion and dream a parent may have for their special son or daughter.

Hope House Children's Hospices provide practical and emotional support to families facing the pain of losing their precious child. We are a hand to hold and a shoulder to cry on no matter what time of day or night so that families can make the most of the time they have left. No charge is ever made to the families who use our service.

We need to raise over £3.8 million annually to ensure the running of both our hospices, Hope House in Oswestry and Tŷ Gobaith in Conwy, including the cost of our extensive social work, counselling and community nursing services. We receive a limited amount of statutory funding – voluntary income is therefore essential to ensure the continuation of the service.

"I can't imagine a more beautiful place to come to terms with the worst possible news," said one mother whose son visits Tŷ Gobaith. "It gives us chance to breathe and to be an ordinary family with our other children. I don't know what we would do without Tŷ Gobaith."

JACK THE STATION CAT
TAKES CHARGE

"C-r-e-e-e-a-k, C-r-e-e-e-a-k," the door of the Station Master's office at Tail's End station swung open. "Time to get up, Jack," said Peter the Porter. "Here's your milk." Peter placed the saucer near Jack's basket. Jack's right ear popped up. Then his left ear. He opened one eye. "Bother!" he thought, "I was having such a nice dream... Bother! Bother! I can't remember what it was about." He shut his eye. He tried very hard, but the dream would not come back.

He tried very hard, but the dream would not come back.

"Come along, Dear Boy," boomed a voice. Aunty Buzz, the retired Station Cat, waddled into the office. "The Royal Train's coming in a few days. Lots to do. Up you get!"

Jack snuggled further into his basket. "I don't want to get up," he grumbled.

"Avast there, ye landlubber! Shake yourself!" Cousin Tom, a retired Sailor Cat, rolled up. "Out of your hammock or I'll keelhaul you!"

No response from Jack, "Slurp, slurp, slurp!" Jack's ears shot up, both eyes opened, he uncurled himself and shot out of his basket. "**TOM**," he yelled, "you're drinking my milk."

"I thought," slurp, "that would get you up," grinned Tom.

Jack glared at him. He lapped up the rest of the milk very fast.

"Now Jack," purred Aunty Buzz, "Tail's End is your station - but **I** know how to greet royalty. Done it scores of times. There are special rules to observe ... so you must know them."

"O.K., Aunty. When do lessons start?"

"After my morning snooze," replied the old cat.

Shortly after, Mr. Parker the Station Master arrived. "Morning, Jack," he said. "Lots of letters here."

"Lots of letters here."

He opened them one by one. "Here's a strange message," he muttered. "Please lend us Jack the Station Cat. We have a problem with a bad rat. Our cat Twm can't cope. He needs help." The letter was signed 'The Director of Ruthin Old Gaol, North Wales'.

"The royal visit to Tail's End is next week," murmured Mr. Parker. "Still, I think we can lend you to the gaol for a day, Jack. I'll arrange for Vernon the Van Driver to take you there."

Jack purred, though he hadn't the faintest idea what Mr. Parker was saying. He went and sharpened his claws. "Scritch, scratch, scrunge!" Then he and Mr. Parker went to the front of the station and found Vernon and Henry the Tail's End parcels van.

High up under the station roof perched Ozimandius the Owl. He sat very still. "I wonder where Jack is going," he thought. Ozimandius lifted a leg and scratched himself.

"Jack! Jack!" shouted Mr. Parker, "into the van." Brrmmm, brrmmm! Henry the Van rolled away.

"Brrmmm, brrmmm!" Henry the Van rolled away.

"Dear me. How surprising - Jack's gone for a ride. It's not his normal day for that." Ozimandius scratched himself again. "I think I should tell someone."

Gareth the Cornish Railway Snail was sitting on his favourite stone in the station garden. Ozimandius flew down beside him." I have some important news," he hooted. Randolph the Rabbit, who was chewing some grass nearby, pricked up his ears. "Please tell us," he said between mouthfuls.

Ozimandius puffed out his chest and opened his eyes so that they looked like saucers. "Jack the

Station Cat has gone for a ride and it's **NOT HIS DAY.**"

Ozamandius . . . opened his eyes so that they looked like saucers.

"He's been kidnapped" squealed the rabbit. He ran round and round in circles. "Don't panic, don't panic! **Do** something, Gareth."

"Red Alert! Red Alert!" announced Gareth. "I will send a Red Alert by E.S.P. " (Electronic Snail Post) "to all Station Snails throughout Britain." He disappeared into his shell. Red lights flashed. The shell turned orange. From inside muffled shouts could be heard. A purple flare shot out of the shell mouth. Then Gareth's head appeared. "Sent off a Red Alert," he wheezed. "But I forgot why."

"Jack's been **KIDNAPPED**," shouted Randolph.

"He has been abducted," added Ozimandius.

"Stuff and nonsense!" purred Aunty Buzz, who had come to see what all the fuss was about. "If Jack has gone for a ride with Vernon he'll come back. Foolish creatures!"

B-r-m-m-m, b-r-m-m-m, Henry the Tail's End parcels van with Vernon driving and Jack sitting next to him, entered the yard of Ruthin Old Gaol.

Henry the Tail's End Parcels van . . .
entered the yard of Ruthin Old Gaol.

Standing at the entrance was the Director and a small black and white cat.

"Hello," said the cat. "I'm Twm, the Gaol Cat. Good of you to come to help me."

"So that's why I'm here," thought Jack. Aloud he said, "Hello Twm. I'll do what I can. I can't spend too long here. I'm preparing for a royal visit to my station. What's the problem?"

"A giant rat, a **bad** rat," replied Twm. "This

building's not a gaol now. It's a museum where humans can see what a gaol was like a long time ago. The rat keeps scaring the visitors with loud squeals and ghostly scratching noises. My human, the Prison Director, is worried in case visitors are frightened away."

"Right!" said Jack. "Let's go and deal with this rat."

The cats went through the main door past the shop. They had just started down a corridor when out of a dark corner a shape appeared. "E-e-e-e-h!" it screamed. "Begone, foul felines!" A second later a piece of mouldy cheese came through the air and hit Jack on the nose.

**A second later a piece of mouldy cheese
came through the air.**

"G-r-r-r-r-r! S-p-i-t-t-z-z! S-p-i-t-t-z-z!" went Jack. "You wretched rat. You will pay for that."

The rat squealed with laughter and vanished. The cats crept slowly down the corridor. Their ears were flat on their heads, their eyes gleamed bright green and their tails twitched.

"Help! Help! Mum! Dad!" two frightened children's voices rang out.

Jack and Twm raced along to the gaol kitchen. On the table were a boy and girl, whilst round it, squeaking loudly, ran a huge rat. "Help us, cats," called the children. Jack and Twm charged at the rat. He shot between them and ran up the corridor shouting "Can't catch me!"

Jack and Twm dashed after him. "He's disappeared again," muttered Jack. "Let's stop and see if we can hear anything."

"Oh dear! Oh dear! No-one likes me!" sobbed a voice nearby.

"There he is," whispered the Gaol Cat.

"What's the matter, Rat?" shouted Jack.

"I'm an actor without a job," cried the rat. "No-one wants me. But I'm good, really I am. Watch me die." He staggered about, fell on the floor, kicked his legs feebly and lay still.

"Watch me die."

"Pretty good," admitted Jack "So if you had a job here you wouldn't be a nuisance. What's your name?"

"I'm called Robbie," replied the rat. "And I'm **not** a nuisance," he added angrily. "I'm showing off my talents as an actor."

The three animals wandered down the corridor. A door was open. "That's the office the Head Gaoler once used," said Twm. "See the toy Gaol Cat asleep on the chair . . . "

". . . and a toy rat trying to steal the gaoler's

meal," squeaked Robbie.

"Wait a minute," thought Jack. He called Twm and Robbie. "Whisper! Whisper! Whisper!"

A little later a party of visitors came along. They held recorded talking guides to their ears.

"Here is the Head Gaoler's office. His cat is on the chair. Not much of a guard cat is he?" asked the recorded voice.

At that moment the cat on the chair slowly got up, jumped off the chair and padded to the table. The rat was busy munching. Occasionally he sat on his hind legs and patted his tummy. Then he licked his lips. He was just starting to wipe his whiskers clean when, with a sudden spring, the cat was on the table.

The rat ran round squealing. The cat growled. Then they both jumped off and disappeared.

. . . with a sudden spring the cat was on the table.

"Radio controlled robots," announced one of the men who was watching.

The party moved on.

"Well done, Twm and Robbie. First class bit of acting," purred Jack.

"Here's another group coming. Get ready."

A second party, accompanied by the Gaol Director, arrived. Twm the Gaol Cat and Robbie performed their playlet. "Wonderful puppetry, Madam Director," said one of the visitors. "Makes everything come alive."

"Er, yes. Thank you . . . ," stuttered the bewildered Director. Then she saw Jack grinning and purring. "Clever, Jack. Thank you," she whispered.

Vernon collected Jack that evening.

"Thank goodness you're back, Dear Boy," purred Aunty Buzz as Jack scampered down the platform.

"You're late!" bellowed Cousin Tom.

"I've been very busy," replied Jack.

The day of the royal visit to Tail's End station arrived. A red carpet was laid out on the platform. At the edge stood Mr. Parker the Station Master, Peter the Porter, Clara the Clerk and Vernon the Van Driver. At the end of the row was Jack. On a station seat nearby sat Aunty Buzz and Cousin Tom. Between them wriggled the twin kittens Marmalade and Myfanwy. In front of a nearby trolley lurked Jack's friend 008, the big black Secret Service Cat. Other Secret Service Cats hid in different places. "Special duties," 008 said to Jack.

"Special duties," 008 said to Jack.

"W-h-e-e-e, w-h-e-e-e!" There was the sound of an engine whistle. In the signal box Sidney the Signalman pulled some levers and "Clang, clang!" off came the signals. The Royal Train drew into the station and stopped exactly by the red carpet. All the people on the platform clapped and cheered. The twin kittens, Marmalade and Myfanwy, were excited. They jumped up and down.

"Be still, Kittens," hissed Aunty Buzz. She

and Tom each put a paw on a kitten.

The Prince and Princess stepped out of the train on to the platform and then shook hands with the station staff. The princess stroked Jack, who PURRED **VERY** loudly.

The Royal Train drew into the station.

Led by Jack the royal couple walked along the platform to the engine.

'Earl of Tail's End' was the engine's name. Her dark green paint and polished brass dome on her boiler gleamed in the sun. Little wisps of steam came from the brass safety valve.

"Thank you, Engine Crew," called the Prince.

"An honour, Sir," replied the driver.

"To what class of engines does 'Earl of Tail's End' belong? asked the Prince.

"She is an old Great Western Railway 'Dukedog'. Some of these engines have always worked in North Wales," replied the driver.

At that point Jack sat in front of the Prince and went "M-i-a-o-o-w-w!"

The driver laughed. "I think Jack wants you and the Princess to go to the station garden. You are planting a tree, I believe."

"My goodness, so we are," replied the Prince. "Goodbye, we had better follow Jack."

The Tail's End station garden looked very pretty in the sun. The beds of flowers were bright with colour and the grass was neatly trimmed. Jack and Mr. Parker led the royal party to one of the beds where a hole had been dug. By the hole were Randolph the Rabbit and his niece Rachel. "Our garden rabbits," said Mr. Parker. "They are friends of Jack."

"I know people who have house rabbits," exclaimed the Princess, "but I've never heard of garden rabbits. Do they do something special?"

"If you would kindly plant this monkey puzzle tree you will see what our garden rabbits can do," was the reply.

Together the Prince and Princess popped the young tree into the hole.

They stood back. Randolph and Rachel started shovelling earth into the hole with their strong back legs. Once the hole was filled the rabbits patted the earth neatly into place.

. . . the rabbits patted the earth neatly into place.

"Your tree is in good hands, I mean 'paws', Your Highnesses," said Mr. Parker. "Station café next," he announced. "Jack the Station Cat will lead the way."

With his tail held high, Jack marched down the platform. As the procession passed their seat Cousin Tom stood on his hind legs and gave a naval salute. Aunty Buzz gave an elegant cat curtsey. The kittens promptly escaped and jumped down on the platform. They rubbed round the Princess's ankles. She picked them up. "Aren't they adorable. Don't be cross with them," she said as she put them back between Aunty Buzz and Cousin Tom.

"Isn't she beautiful?" sighed Myfanwy.

"Even better than a Midnight Mouse," added Marmalade.

The party arrived at the station Tea Rooms. The railway Tea Ladies, Val and Jacq, were waiting for them with cups of tea and cakes. The Prince and Princess talked to Val and Jacq and were introduced to a very special guest.

"Meet Miss Margaret Green, our oldest regular customer," said Val. "She's over 90."

"Pleased to meet you, Your Royal Highnesses. It's such an honour," said Miss Green.

"Nice to meet **you**, Miss Green," replied the Princess. "Do sit down and tell me about your interesting life."

Miss Green was one of Jack's best friends, and he rubbed gently round her ankles when she sat down.

Behind the Princess and Miss Green a pair of curtains hung on part of the café wall. "We would be pleased if you would pull these curtains," said Mr. Parker to the Princess. "There's a plaque behind them recording your visit."

Everybody watched as the Princess took hold of the cord. Nothing happened. "They're a bit heavy," she said. The Prince went to help her. They tugged really hard. The curtains flew back. "M-i-a-a-a-o-w! M-i-a-a-a-o-w!"

There, clinging one to each curtain, were Marmalade and Myfanwy. Everyone cheered, including the Prince and Princess. Two Secret Service cats grabbed the twins and marched them off to one side.

. . . clinging one to each curtain . . .

An official approached. "I'm afraid it is time to go, Your Highnesses. We have an extra call to make," he said. "The Director of Ruthin Old Gaol wants to show you something special. It is Jack the Station Cat's idea. Here comes your helicopter now."

"Chatter, chatter, chatter!" Down came the helicopter into the station yard. Everyone went to say goodbye. Jack, Aunty Buzz and Cousin Tom jumped on the roof of Vernon's van to get a good view. Thump! Thump! Two Secret Service cats - one with Myfanwy on his back, the other with Marmalade - joined them.

"Goodbye, Jack," called the Prince. "Goodbye, kittens," added the Princess. The royal party climbed aboard, and with loud "Chatter, chatter, chatter!" noises the helicopter rose into the sky and disappeared.

"You were a First Class Station Cat, Jack," said Mr. Parker. "Go to the café. You will find a thank-you there."

Jack trotted along to the café . Val appeared.

"Jack," she called, "come here. I've a special treat for a Special Station Cat." It was a bowl of lovely thick creamy yoghurt. Jack lapped contentedly. "Treated like royalty myself," he purred.

Jack lapped contentedly.

THE END

Dear Boys & Girls...

There really is an Old Gaol at Ruthin in North Wales. It is a museum and if you go there you will find Twm the Gaol Cat and Robbie the Rat. They are toys though. I wonder if you can think of a way to make them work.

When a train carrying royalty arrives at a station it is a matter of professional pride that the driver stops exactly at the spot where the red carpet is. It is not easy - especially with a steam engine.

There is one real 'Dukedog' locomotive left. You will find it on the Bluebell Railway which runs from Sheffield Park through Horsted Keynes to Kingscote near East Grinstead in Sussex. The loco's number is 9017 and its name 'Earl of Berkeley'. Years ago it ran in North Wales and was shedded at Machynlleth. If you see the engine give the driver a wave from Jack.

Alan Cliff

PUZZLES

1) Jack may later have written the sentence below, but he forgot to put any spaces between the words. Can you make sense of it?

Ihadaveryexcitingdaywhentheredcarpetwaslaidoutonthe platformfortheroyalvisit.

2) Which two cats are retired?

3) Complete the following:

(a) Prince and _ _ _ _ _ _ _ _

(b) _ _ _ _ and Queen

(c) _ _ _ _ and Duchess

(d) Lord and _ _ _ _

4) **You can put at least 10 individual letters of the alphabet before   AT to make 3-letter words.**
e.g. C A T
R A T

But when you say the words, one of them does not rhyme with the others. Which one is that?

5) **What do these have in common?**

(a) The helicopter and Ozamandius.
They both

(b) The Gaol Director and the Princess.
They were both

(c) The Alert sent by Gareth and the Carpet on the platform.
Both were

6) **A MONKEY PUZZLE TREE** when 10 years old is about 152cms (or 5 ft.) tall.
It grows to 14 times that height.
How tall will it be when fully grown?

(A Monkey Puzzle Tree has branches that look like thick ropes. Someone said "It would be a puzzle for a monkey to climb that tree!")

7)   a) How many cats were on top of Vernon's van when the
        Prince and Princess were leaving Tail's End?

        b) Which was the other cat <u>not</u> with them but which was
        named in the story?

        c) Which cat on the same roof had the same name as Answer
        (b) but his name was the English translation of it?

8)   Who were the two humans who especially thanked Jack for
        his help?

ANSWERS

1) I had a very exciting day when the red carpet was laid out on the platform for the royal visit.

2) Aunty Buzz and Cousin Tom.

3) (a) Princess (b) King (c) Duke (d) Lady

4) **EAT**

5) (a) flew (b) female (ladies) (c) red

6) 5 x 14 = 70 ft or 152 x 14 = 2128 cms/21 metres, 28 cms.

7) a) 7 b) Twm c) Tom (Cousin Tom)

8) Gaol Director and Mr. Parker